LOVE LETTERS AND OTHER STORIES

SHORT STORIES BY

KATE WALKER

JANE YOLEN

HEIDI ELISABET YOLEN STEMPLE

GLORIA D. MIKLOWITZ

NORMA FOX MAZER

SCHOLASTIC INC.

New York   Toronto   London   Auckland   Sydney
Mexico City   New Delhi   Hong Kong

COVER ILLUSTRATION BY
TIM BARRALL

ILLUSTRATIONS BY
SHAWN BANNER

"Love Letters" © 1988 by Kate Walker was first published in
State of the Heart, compiled by P.E. Matthews (Omnibus Books © 1988).
"Opening Act" © 1995 by Jane Yolen and Heidi Elisabet Yolen Stemple was first published
in *Scholastic SCOPE*® magazine, Vol. 43, No. 12, February 3, 1995.
"My Side of the Story" © 1991 by Gloria D. Miklowitz was first published
in *Scholastic SCOPE*® magazine, Vol. 40, No. 4, October 4, 1991.
"Calling Jack Kettle" © 1995 by Norma Fox Mazer was first published in
Scholastic SCOPE® magazine, Vol. 43, No. 13, February 10, 1995.

5   6   7   8   9   10   23   06   05   04

TABLE of CONTENTS

LOVE LETTERS

KATE WALKER

My name's Nick, and my girlfriend's name is Fleur. And she has a friend called Helen who's got a boyfriend named Clive. Now this Clive is really weird. Well, he does one weird thing I know of anyway. He writes three-page letters to his girlfriend, Helen, *every* day.

"What's wrong with the nerd?" I asked Fleur. She'd spent a whole lunch time telling me about him.

"There's nothing *wrong* with him," she said. "You're so unromantic, Nick."

"Of course I'm not unromantic!" I said, and I offered her a lick of my ice cream to prove it. She groaned and pulled her gym bag over her head. She didn't want to talk to me any more.

When girls go quiet, that's a bad sign.

"What's wrong?" I asked her.

"You don't love me," she said.

"Of course I love you," I told her. I offered her my whole ice cream. She wouldn't take it.

"You don't love me *enough*," she said.

"How much is *enough*?"

How much ice cream did it take?

"You don't write *me* letters like Clive does to Helen," she said.

"I don't need to. I see you every day in computer class," I said. "*And* chemistry."

"Clive sees Helen every day in biology, math, and homeroom," she said, "and he writes letters to *her*!"

I knew what was happening here. My girlfriend was cooling on me.

"Okay," I said, "I'll write you a letter."

"Aw, Nick!" She whipped her gym bag off her head.

I was glad I'd weakened. Fleur is really gorgeous. I couldn't risk losing her for the sake of a few lines scrawled on a piece of paper.

I sat down that night and began my first letter: "Dear Fleur. . . ." Then I stared at the page for the next half hour. What do you write in letters to someone you see every day? I chewed my pencil. I chewed my nails. Then, in desperation, I finally asked Mom.

"Write about the things you have in common," Mom said, so I wrote the following: "Wasn't that computer class on Tuesday funny? The best part was when Brando tilted the computer to show us the little button underneath and the monitor fell off."

I wrote about the chemistry class too, though it wasn't quite as interesting. Not a single kid messed up their experiment.

The next day, I got the letter back with "D-" marked on the bottom.

"What was wrong with it?" I asked Fleur.

"You made a lot of spelling mistakes for one thing," she said.

"I was being *myself*!" I told her.

"I didn't notice," she said. "You didn't say anything *personal* in it!"

Is that what she wanted, a *personal* letter?

I thought it over for five minutes. There were guys all around the lunch area just waiting to take my place and share their chocolate milk with the fabulous Fleur. If revealing a few personal secrets was what it took to keep her, I could do it.

"Dear Fleur, . . ." I began the second letter that night. "This is not something I'd tell everyone, but I use deodorant. Only on gym day or in really hot weather, of course."

No, that was too personal. I ripped up the page and started again. "Dear Fleur, Guess what? Mrs. Hessel blew up at me in history today for no reason at all. I was embarrassed to death. Goggle-eyes Gilda laughed her stupid head off."

Actually, once I started, I found the personal stuff not that hard to write. I told Fleur what mark I *really* got on the English midterm. Then I told her about a movie I'd seen where this pioneer guy loses his plow horse, then loses his wife, then his children, and then his cows get hoof rot. But even though he sits down and bawls his eyes out about it, in the end he walks off into the sunset, a stronger man.

"I'd like to suffer a great personal loss like that," I told Fleur in the letter, "and walk away stronger and nobler for it."

Her sole comment on letter number two was: "You didn't say anything in it about *me*." And she went off to eat lunch with Helen.

It was time to hit the panic button. Fleur was drifting away from me. I stuffed my sandwiches back in my bag and went looking for Clive. I cornered him under the stairwell.

"Okay, what do you put in your letters to Helen?" I asked him.

Clive turned out to be a decent kid. He not only told me, he gave me a photocopy of the latest letter he was writing to Helen.

You should have seen it!

"Darling Helen, Your hair is like gold. Your eyes remind me of twilight reflected on Throsby Creek. Your ear lobes are . . . Your eyelashes are . . ." And so on. It was what you'd call a poetic autopsy.

And as if that wasn't bad enough, he then got into the declarations of love: "You're special to me because. . . I yearn for you in history because . . . I can't eat noodles without thinking of you because . . ."

"Do girls really go for this mushy sort of thing?" I asked him.

"Helen does," he said. "She'd drop me tomorrow if I stopped writing her letters. It's the price you pay if you want to keep your girlfriend."

So I began my third letter, with Clive's photocopy propped up in front of me as a guide.

"Dear Fleur, Your hair is like . . ." I began.

Actually, I'd always thought it was pretty from a distance but gooey when you touched it—too much gel?

I scrapped that opening and started again.

"Dear Fleur, Your eyes are like . . ."

Actually, they're a bit small and squinty. I think she might need glasses.

Forget the eyes.

"Dear Fleur, Your face is excellent overall. You look like one of those soap opera actresses."

I thought I would have been able to go on for hours about her face, but having said that, it seemed to sum her up.

I moved on to the declarations: "I love you because . . ." I chewed my pencil again, then my fingernails. This time I couldn't ask Mom.

Why did I love Fleur? Because she was spunky. Because all the guys thought so, too. Well, not all of them. Some of them thought she wasn't all that interesting to talk to, but I put that down to jealousy.

Still, I began to wonder, what *had* we talked about in the three weeks we'd been going together? Not much really. She'd never been interested enough in my hockey playing to ask in-depth questions about it. And, I have to admit, I hadn't found her conversation on white ankle boots all that riveting either.

No wonder I was having so much trouble writing

letters to her. We had nothing in common. I barely knew her. What were her views on nuclear waste disposal? Was she for or against the death penalty?

I scrapped the letter, scrapped Clive's photocopy, and started again, this time with no trouble at all.

"Dear Fleur, This writing of letters was a very good idea because it gives me the opportunity to say something important to you. I think you're a nice girl, and I've enjoyed going out with you for three weeks, but I think we should call it off. Even if it's a great personal loss to both of us, I'm sure we'll walk away stronger and nobler. Yours sincerely, Nick."

I slipped the letter to her in computer class. She didn't take it too badly. She just ripped it up. But then two days later photocopies of my *personal* letter started to circulate around the school.

I didn't mind, though, because as a result of that, Goggle-eyes Gilda slipped me a note in history that said, briefly: "I like your style, Nick. You've got depth." I took another look at Goggle-eyes. I didn't mind her style either. She has this terrific laugh, and she's a whiz on computers.

I wrote back right away, my own kind of letter this time—honest and to the point: "Dear Gilda, That three-minute talk you gave on speech day about Third World famine relief was really excellent. I'll be eating lunch at noon if you'd care to join me."

Opening Act

JANE YOLEN AND

HEIDI ELISABET YOLEN STEMPLE

Well, she's not exactly famous. More like well known. At least if you live in our county you'd know her name. Probably you'd have heard her sing at church or at somebody's wedding.

She won the grand prize on a show like *Star Search* about ten years ago, before there even was a *Star Search*—when I was small enough to think that was a big deal. I must have watched the tape Daddy made of the show a hundred times. But to tell the truth, it's real embarrassing now. The songs about love gone wrong and how another guy dumped her.

Once I asked how she would even know what being dumped felt like when she's been married to Daddy for about a million years. I mean sometimes they still act like teenagers. She just laughed and said it was a feeling no one ever forgets.

Ever since I can remember, everyone has always asked me if I wanted to be a singer like my mom when I grow up. Mom used to take me onstage with her. When I was three and four and five years old, I guess it was cute. But when it got painful—for both the audience and me—she stopped. One day I was the star of the family, the next day I was nothing. I didn't understand, really, till I turned twelve and was kicked out of the school choir. Seems I can't carry a tune. Not even in a bucket loader.

I guess I have my dad's genes when it comes to music. He left Woodstock and became an accountant. Anyway, these days I can't even imagine how terrifying it must be to get up and sing in front of people. I think I'd rather be an accountant, not that anyone ever asks about that.

On the other hand, my older brother Aaron is a bigger ham than Mom. He has his own band in Minneapolis, and he sings, plays guitar, even writes his own music. He's the real star. Mom walks around the house humming his tunes. My dad, Mr. "I only listen to country music," even abandoned his Willie Nelson CDs for Aaron's newest tape. And sometimes I catch myself singing his songs as well, with my voice!

Maybe I can't sing, but I do know about the kind of heartbreak in my mom's songs—which brings me to my reason for telling this story. Right after school started this fall, I heard from some "friend" that my boyfriend, Jeff, had been eyeing Marie McCall.

I had never liked the way he looked at her in the school hallways between classes. But a lot of boys looked at Marie that way, especially now because she changed quite a bit over summer vacation—and I didn't.

Since Jeff hadn't called me since school started, I suspected that meant we were breaking up after a summer together, though I hoped I was wrong.

However, the last thing that I would have done was to get up onstage and sing about it. *As summer slipped into the fall, you dumped me for Marie McCall.* What a catchy tune.

I've always thought the best way to deal with heartbreak was to write poetry in secret. Better than singing about fake heartbreak on a stage anyway. Like the twenty-seven poems I wrote about Brian, my last boyfriend, who moved to Texas when his mom was offered a great job there. I keep those poems safely tucked away in a box in the back of my closet. After all, they're no one's business but my own.

When the phone rang last week at ten-thirty, I jumped to answer it. I was up studying for my math test and my parents were watching TV. I knew, in that way that you just know, that the phone was for me. Sure enough, it was my best friend, Kaytlin. She had been at the mall, not needing to study, because she isn't in an advanced anything class.

"Manda," she said, out of breath. "This couldn't wait till morning. It's too important." There was an edge to her voice I couldn't quite grasp. "Are you ready? Are you sitting down?"

"Yes," I said, although I wasn't.

"Manda, it's Jeff. I saw him with Marie McCall."

That's when I sat down. "They were coming out of the movies together, and I followed them."

Although there was nothing funny about this, I almost smiled. Kaytlin wants to be a police officer like her father and three older brothers, and she tends to act as if she were already undercover.

"Were you lurking?" I asked.

I could just see her pulling her jacket up around her face and sneaking about. Sometimes I am jealous that she knows exactly what she wants to be.

"After about half an hour of surveillance . . . are you sure you're sitting?"

I made an affirmative sound.

"He kissed her."

Suddenly I didn't want any more details. "Kate, I've got to go. My mom is calling me," I lied. I'm sure she knew I wasn't telling the truth.

I abandoned my books and ran upstairs. I hate crying, really. But it seemed the right thing to do. So I did, into my pillow, where no one could hear me.

After I'd cried as much as I could, I started writing in my poetry journal. I was inspired. Heartbreak does that to me. And the rhymes had nothing to do with Marie or McCall. Or Jeff either. It had to do with me. And with poetry.

I'm picking up the pieces of my heart
First you mended it, then tore it all apart
You've made despair an art form
And cheating an art.

I was feeling better in a strange sort of way. I'd read somewhere that many poets find poetry a catharsis. I could definitely understand that. So, I continued:

You tore down my palace and my throne,
The ones I'd built of mortar and of bone.
You razed it piece by piece,
Each precious little stone.

I loved that word "razed," the way it made me feel.

I wrote for another hour or so. Crossing lines out, rewriting the rhymes. It always happens that way. The first stanza or two come quickly, but the following ones need to be worked and reworked. As I wrote, the writing itself became my entire universe, rhyme and meter replacing tears and pain.

When I was done, I reread the whole poem aloud. I was happy with it—and exhausted.

I must have fallen asleep, because the next moment it was morning and I was still in my clothes. But, curiously, someone had tucked me neatly under the covers. And the lights were off.

My journal, however, was nowhere to be found. Worrying about my math test and wondering what could have happened to my journal, I went downstairs to breakfast.

When I got there, my dad was reading the financial section of the paper, as usual. Mom was sipping her tea. It seemed normal enough until I spotted my poetry notebook right by her bread plate, covered with crumbs from her toast.

I snatched up the notebook and screamed. For all I knew, they'd been having a good laugh at my expense over their breakfast of cereal and toast.

"Manda, honey," Mom began, "these are—"

I cut her off, too mad to hear her excuses. Or worse—her criticisms of my work. "You had no right to violate my privacy!"

I squeaked. I always squeak when I am really angry, which sort of undercuts the effect. Turning, I stomped out, slamming the door behind me. That made a great punctuation, like one enormous exclamation point. I was halfway to school before I realized I had left without my books or jacket. And to make things worse, I was early for school.

My anger brewed through first-period civics. My stomach growled through the second-period math test. By the time I reached lunch, I had decided that not speaking to my mother was the only way to deal with her. She might *read* my words, but I sure wasn't going to let her *hear* them. I was so mad, I forgot to be heartbroken, till I saw Jeff walking hand in hand with Marie McCall. Then it all flooded back.

"I don't know who I hate worse," I told Kaytlin.

"What do you mean?" she asked.

"My mom or Jeff. They both broke faith with me," I said.

"I thought Jeff broke your heart," she said.

"Whatever."

I didn't want to talk any more to Kaytlin. She just didn't get it. What I really wanted to do was call my brother, Aaron, but he was on tour with his band. However, since they were headed our way for a Friday night gig at the Iron Horse Cafe, three days away, I supposed I could hold out until after the show. I might not want to talk to Mom, and I couldn't talk to Kaytlin, but—boy—was Aaron going to get an earful!

The three long days until Friday seemed closer to a year and a half, but somehow I made it through.

Mom tried several times to talk to me. Once in the kitchen, she stopped me in the middle of making a peanut butter sandwich and said: "Manda, your poem is . . ." And once at the dinner table she began: "Honey, you've got to let me . . ." But I walked out each time, letting the door slams be double exclamation points. She got the message and left me alone. Just maybe, I thought, she knew she was wrong. Just maybe, I thought, I'd stop being mad a year from now.

Even Dad tried to get into the act, saying: "Your mom thought the notebook was homework, Manda. It's a terrific poem and . . ."

And I cut him off too, saying: "She sings about broken hearts. I live them. I don't want to talk about it." So we didn't.

To make things easier, Mom had nightly rehearsals with her group, as they were the opening act for Aaron's band. So every night when she got home, I was already in bed. I pretended I was already asleep.

And then—suddenly—it was Friday. I was so excited to see my brother, I didn't mind having to listen to Mom's group first. She had already left for her sound check, so Daddy and I drove over together talking about everything: the new pizza parlor in town, my math test, my brother's band. Everything, in fact, except my fight with Mom. Daddy was too diplomatic to bring that up again. Came from dealing with crazed clients at tax season, I guess.

At the Iron Horse, we were given the best table in the house and treated like the family of royalty, which, on this night, I guess we were. The owner of the club, who called himself Mom's "biggest fan," came to our table twice to make sure we were comfortable.

Finally, the lights dimmed, and it was time for Mom to take the stage. At other times, I had found this a magic moment, the lights going down, her name called over the speakers, the applause, and then her entrance. But I was still too mad at her to let the magic work. And for the first time it all seemed a little—I don't know—cheap, maybe?

She started her set with a loud jazzy number that got the entire audience clapping in time with the beat. I didn't clap on principle. After all, she was still the woman who had stolen my journal and read my most secret poetry.

After watching Mom for a while, I had to admit,

she looked wonderful in her white gauzy dress, and she sounded great, too. So maybe a little bit of the magic still worked. I couldn't help but tap my foot to the beat of the music. When I realized what I was doing, I made myself stop.

Then, she pulled up a stool and sat for a sad ballad that cried out for a lost boyfriend, long gone, but not forgotten. As usual, it made me blush. But something more, too. It made me think about Jeff and how he had left me for Marie McCall. I let the lyrics wash over me, tell me my own story. And—you know—I felt better. Other people had suffered before and it wasn't the end of the world. Maybe that's what music does best—reminds us that we are like other people.

Mom sang three more songs and then finished with an old lullaby. She used to sing that song to me whenever I was sick or scared of the dark. This time she sang it with a slight blues beat and it seemed—somehow—like a kind of apology. Then she blew kisses to the audience, acknowledged her band, bowed, and turned to go.

This was a trick I had seen many times before. She wasn't ready to leave yet; she knew the audience would yell for just one more song. Even though I knew it was a practiced routine, she seemed believable when she turned and slowly walked back to the microphone.

"As many of you know," Mom started, her voice low, "tonight is a very special night for me. My son's band is patiently awaiting our departure from the stage so they can come out and show you their stuff."

I could feel the excitement building and had to admire the way she controlled the audience. Even I was excited.

"But, what I know that you all don't know—and I wasn't even fully aware of until this very week—is that he isn't my only talented child."

I heard my mother's words, but didn't quite get it. Call me slow, but I was waiting for Aaron to come on.

"Amanda, honey, could you join me onstage?" I heard my name, and suddenly there was a spotlight on me and my dad was pulling me to my feet. I stood up, feeling as if I were in a haze. I looked at my mother, who was motioning to me.

I was really angry at Mom for embarrassing me in front of all these people. But that anger was small compared to my overwhelming fear. I hadn't been up onstage in ten years. She couldn't possibly mean for me to go up there. And do what? Sing? With my voice?

Then Daddy gave me a push from behind and my feet seemed to move on their own. I walked, shaking all the way, onto the stage.

Mom hugged me, though I was stiff with anger and fear. I smiled a weak smile and attempted a feeble escape, but she led me to the empty stool, where she sat me down. Then she began talking again. I only made out parts of what she was saying.

". . . which she wrote . . . doesn't know . . . music . . . apology . . . hope you like it as much as . . ."

And as I sat, red-faced and shaking, her backup group started to play a slow, sad melody.

When she sang the opening lines, I could hardly believe it.

I'm picking up the pieces of my heart; first you mended it, and then tore it apart. You've made despair an art form, and cheating an art. I'm picking up the pieces of my heart.

After the first stanza, she looked at me and smiled. My face must have registered shock and horror, because she moved closer while the band played an instrumental section. Then she picked up my limp right hand and her eyes told me to look out into the crowd. I looked. It was better than staring at her. I could only see a couple of rows into the darkened café.

You tore down my palace and my throne . . .

As she started singing again, my dad's face was the first I focused on. He had an awfully odd expression. I couldn't tell if there was a kind of feedback from the spotlight, but he almost seemed to have tears in his eyes. I may have started to smile.

The ones I'd built of mortar and of bone.

I looked past him to strangers in the audience. They were swaying to the music. Now I know I was smiling.

You took it down slow piece by piece. Each precious little stone.

I looked just offstage to my right. Aaron and the guys in his band were all watching and listening. And grinning. I grinned back. I just couldn't help it.

24

You tore down my palace and my throne.

Mom squeezed my hand. I closed my eyes while she finished the song.

Our song.

When the music ended, I opened my eyes again. Everyone was clapping and cheering. One by one they began to stand. Mom released my hand and took a bow. Then she turned to me and pulled me up by the shoulders to stand beside her.

"Razed," I whispered. "Razed it piece by piece. You changed my words. How could you?"

"Words on a page," she whispered back, "are different than words in the mouth. Trust me on this one, sweetie. Now bow. The applause—it's for you."

I looked for my brother, but he had disappeared. Only his band remained, clapping right along with the crowd. Suddenly I realized what Mom had said. I was supposed to bow. So I tried. But have you ever bowed when your knees are shaking with anger? And with joy? All I managed was some sort of bob.

All at once, the audience got very excited. They roared even louder this time. So I bowed again, this time a deep one. When I came up from my bow, Aaron was there with a bouquet of red roses. He handed them to me and kissed my cheek.

"So," he said, "you've been holding out on me, Sis. And me struggling along with my own lousy lyrics. You going to write me something, too?"

"You can't sing about heartbreak," I said. "I happen

to know that no one has ever dumped you."

"I sing about lots of things that never happened to me," he said.

"What about razing?" I asked.

He laughed. He didn't know what I was talking about, but it didn't matter. "Up or down?" he asked. Then he laughed again. "Now get off the stage. It's my turn now."

As I sat next to Daddy, I thought: "You raised me up, I razed you down. . . ." It was the start of a song and Aaron could sing it. Or Mom. Whatever.

GLORIA D. MIKLOWITZ

Cassie

"Cass! How nice to see you again!" Janet, Dad's new wife, opens the door. She wears old jeans and an oversized shirt and carries a mostly bald baby. Her son, Paul, stands beside her, a superior smirk on his face.

Dad had remarried and moved to another state so I only saw him when he came to Los Angeles on business. Until now. Now he's moved back, bought a house for his new family, and wants me to visit every other weekend.

"Come in, come in, Cass!" Janet says. She holds the baby like a shield, the way I'm holding the tennis racket and my stuffed animal Eeyore. "Paul! Take Cass's bag to the baby's room. James? James honey? Cass is here!"

Dad storms into the room holding a big packing box. He sets it down and spreads his arms wide, "Cass, sweetheart! Come here and give your old dad a hug!"

He's the same dad, with the same happy grin for me, but with them around, it's not the same. I let Dad hug me, the donkey and racket between us.

"My goodness!" He draws back, keeping an arm around my shoulder. "You haven't met the most important member of our family yet, your baby sister!"

Janet turns so I can see Sabina on her shoulder. The baby has big hazel eyes, like Dad's, a pretty mouth, and rosy cheeks. "Ah ga!" she says to me.

"Want to hold her?"

I know what Janet's trying to do. "No thanks. I'd like to go to my room now, please."

"Sure honey," Dad says. "Just follow Paul, and as soon as you're settled, come out to the back and we'll have a cool drink together."

I hear their low voices as I follow Paul down the hall to the baby's room. Are they talking about me, I wonder. Paul opens the door to a small room with a crib and single bed. "Sabina doesn't cry anymore at night, so she shouldn't wake you." He tosses my bag on the bed and looks at me with a silly grin that puts me on guard. "Tell me. The way you hold on to that stuffed animal, I'm wondering—is it part of you?"

I open my mouth, then close it. "That's my father's jogging suit you're wearing!" I cry with as much meanness as I feel. "I gave that to him for Christmas!"

"Yeah? Which Christmas?"

I have to think. "Three years ago!"

"Here, then!" He starts to peel off the top. The smile is gone.

"Get out of here!" I drop Eeyore and push Paul out the door. "I hate you! I hate you all! I didn't want to come!" I slam the door and fall on the bed. A whole weekend with strangers! I came to see Dad, not Janet or Paul or that bald baby!

"Cassie? Sweetheart?" Dad knocks at the door. "We're waiting. Janet's baked some chocolate nut cookies just for you!" When I don't answer, Dad calls, "Here I come, ready or not!" and opens the door. He sits on the bed, but I turn away. "I know it's hard for you, honey," he says, "but give us a chance. Maybe when we get better settled, you and I can play tennis, take a walk, or something. Okay? Now come outside and join the fun."

They look so cozy around the picnic table. Janet turns her face up for Dad's kiss. Paul holds the baby, who's chewing happily on plastic keys. When she sees me she says, "Ah ga!"

"She likes you!" Janet says, passing me a glass of apple juice.

"Aren't Janet's cookies fabulous?" Dad asks.

I nod to please him.

"Remember those peanut butter squares I tried on you guys?" Janet chuckles. "We had to eat them with a spoon."

"Remember the popcorn I made when I forgot to put the lid on the pot?" Paul asks.

"Remember . . ."

I look from one to the other as they share memories I'm not a part of, and I feel left out.

After a while Dad says, "Time to get back to work."

He picks up the glasses to bring back to the kitchen. "We still have lots of unpacking to do. Cassie, want to give me a hand?"

I'm about to say, "Sure, Dad!" when Janet cries, "Oh, no, James, please! I can't do a thing with Sabina around! Cassie's so good with babies, you said. Could she possibly take over for an hour or two?"

"What do you say, Cassie?" Dad asks. "It would really help."

I swallow disappointment and say, "Sure, okay."

Paul plunks the baby in my arms and takes off after Dad. Janet thanks me, kisses the baby, and says, "You're a good sport, Cassie. I'll be in the kitchen if you need me."

Sabina leans away from me, watching her mother disappear. She starts to whimper and her eyes fill with doubt and fear. Why should I trust you, she seems to be wondering. And then her little mouth curls into a worried pout and she's crying.

"Come on now, Bina," I whisper, jiggling her up and down. "Don't cry. We'll have fun. It's okay. I'm your sister!" I jiggle her some more and sing "Twinkle Twinkle" and "Old MacDonald," but she doesn't care. She cries like her heart is broken.

I carry her into the house looking for help, but Janet's on a ladder lining shelves and Dad's fixing a towel rack and Paul's in the garage, bringing in more boxes to unpack.

I take her to the room we share and lie on my bed

with my arms wrapped around her little body. Her legs feel so new and soft, and she smells so sweet, like sunshine. I make up a song about me and her and our best friend, Eeyore. Soon she forgets I'm a stranger and pulls at Eeyore's nose and tail and tastes his ragged ear. "Ah ga?" she asks, head tipped sideways, and I have to laugh.

That's when Paul comes in and says Janet wants me to help him pick lemons. Why? Does it take two people to pick a couple of lemons?

I deliver Sabina to Janet and go out to the yard. Wouldn't you know—Paul hides in the tree and throws a lemon at me! Fifteen years old, going on ten!

"James is going to build a treehouse for Sabina!" he says. Boy, that hurts! "Dad's buying me a car for my birthday."

Dad? Dad? How dare he call *my father* "Dad," like they're close or something? I can't stand him another second and run into the house.

Dinnertime, he doesn't look at me. He's angry that Janet and I are getting along and were laughing in the kitchen when he came in. Janet was telling about her first kiss and how she couldn't figure out what to do with her nose. He wanted to know what was funny, but she wouldn't say.

At dinner he's mad at Dad for talking about his old girlfriend, for asking me to give him advice about making new friends, and for hurting his macho image. He storms off to his room, and I roll my eyes and think,

"What a baby!" It's nice with him gone.

Dad tells Janet about some of the fun things we used to do. Janet tells how she first met Dad when she loaned him a quarter for a parking meter, and he tracked her down to pay it back. When we're cleaning up the pizza mess, Janet says, "Paul's in a sulk. His male ego's been hurt. You know how guys are. They think they can solve all the world's problems alone."

Dad clears his throat, and I think Janet's talking about him, too.

"Anyway," Janet says, "I hate for him to feel left out. I could go talk to him, or James could, but maybe if you went . . ."

"Let him be," Dad says. "He'll get over it."

"It's hard on him, too, James," Janet says.

"I'll go," I say, wanting to please Janet. I go to Paul's room and knock, but don't know what I'll say. I only know how he must feel. He doesn't want to talk to me, of course, but when I apologize for making trouble between him, his mom, and my dad, he's suddenly listening to me.

I think, without saying, how I didn't want to come for this weekend because I wouldn't belong. Well, I don't yet, but I see the possibility. I want to say, "Paul— you already belong. Let me, too." Instead I say, "I guess I've got to get along with all of you if I want time with my dad. That's all I came to say."

Something in his face changes even as I turn away. I don't know why. He grabs my arm. Suddenly, he's nice, invites me into his room, puts on a tape, asks me about the high school he'll be going to.

And suddenly—I don't know how—we're talking.

Paul

Oh man! What a baby! There she stood at the door. Cassie—my stepsister, visiting for the first time for a weekend. Looking like she'd just been shown into the dentist's office to have all her teeth pulled. I'm in total disbelief. Thirteen years old and she's still hugging a stuffed animal?

"I expect you to be nice to her," Mom had said. "She's James's daughter and it's got to be hard on her, coming here, especially when we're so busy getting settled in our new home."

"*Poor baby . . .*" I said.

"Stop that!" Mom gave me a nasty look. "Your stepfather has been very good to you, Paul. You'll show your appreciation by helping Cassie feel comfortable!"

So, okay. I give it a shot. I join the greeting party at the door. I play bellboy and bring her bag to her room. And then—just to test the water—I make a joke about the donkey she hangs onto for dear life. Wow! Out come the fangs and I'm out of there like a light!

Fifteen minutes later James has unglued her from that thing she carries and lured her outside. We've got home-baked cookies in her honor. We've put a cloth on the picnic table. We've taken time out from all the work we've got to do. Is she into it? No way!

34

ches Mom like maybe she's a serial killer, eye like a starving person looking in a bakery wind she doesn't look at me at all. When we get back to work, Mom asks if Cassie could watch Sabina. I see the mental wheels spinning. "Is that why I'm here? To be a baby-sitter all weekend!"

I get a special kick putting Sabina in her arms. Who knows? A couple of hours with Bina and maybe she won't come again. Which wouldn't break my heart. Who needs a girl to share the bathroom with? Besides, my stepdad and I get along pretty well now. Who needs the competition?

"Bring me some lemons from the tree out back, Paul," Mom says a while later. "Take Cassie along."

"All right," I say and trot off to the baby's room. The door's partly open and I hear Cass singing, so I go right in. Sabina's sitting on my stepsister's lap, happily chewing on that old stuffed donkey with its thirteen years of germs.

Cassie looks up. For a second she's got the same sweet expression Sabina gets sometimes, but then she sees me. Her eyes turn dark and distant.

"Mom says it's time for Sabina's dinner," I say. "She wants us to pick some lemons. Meet me out back." I turn around before she can show her fangs.

The lemon tree is old, like the house, and most of the lemons are rotting on the ground. I climb up on a limb to reach some of the better ones and see Cass coming across the lawn.

"Paul? Paul?" she calls, looking for me.

"Catch!" I throw a lemon towards her. It almost hits her, and she jumps. It scares her, which isn't what I meant to do.

We sit on opposite limbs kind of looking and not looking at each other. I pick a lemon and hold it to my nose. She swings her legs and checks out the view.

"I'm sorry I screamed at you before," she says.

"I'm sorry I teased you," I say.

She plucks a lemon, smells it, and takes a bite without flinching. I'm thinking she's not such a bad kid after all if she has the guts to apologize.

"We had a house too," she says, wistfully. "We had two dogs and a cat and a swimming pool and twenty rose bushes." She brightens when she adds, "Dad taught me to play tennis, and when I was younger, he built me a treehouse!"

"James says he'll build a treehouse for Sabina when she's big enough." My words wound, though I don't mean them to. Worse, I add, "Dad's buying me a car for my birthday!"

"*Your* dad's buying you a car?"

"No! Dad—you know, James!"

There's fire in her eyes when she says, "He's not *your* dad! Don't call him that! You have a father! Dad is *mine*!"

"Psssssh!"

She bites her lip and turns away. "Shouldn't we be picking lemons?" She plucks two, then drops to the

37

ground with a thud and heads into the house.

I almost feel sorry for her until I think—why? She's a snake. If I'm nice, she'll only want to hang around me whenever she comes.

Mom sends me off to the store. When I walk into the kitchen later with the pizza for dinner, Cassie's at the sink, washing salad stuff and giggling. "What's funny?" I ask. Mom exchanges giggly looks with Cass and says, "Girl talk." There's silence until I leave, then the giggling starts again. I don't like it. This is my house, my mom!

"Paul's worried about going to a new high school," James says at dinner. "It's hard on him—leaving all his old friends—even a *girlfriend*. Right, pal?" James winks at me.

I feel like he's punched me in the gut, reminding me about Tina and school, making me look wimpy in front of my stepsister. "Hey James, I'm *not* worried," I say.

Cassie eyes me with interest. "When we moved after the divorce, I had to go to another school, too. It was hard to fit in."

"Do you have any suggestions to make it easier for him?" Mom asks.

"Hey, cut it out, all of you! I can manage my own life!" I cry.

"No one said you couldn't, Paul. But if Cassie can help . . ." Mom says.

"Oh, sure! Some help she could give. She'll probably say, 'Take your teddy bear along!'"

I'm in big trouble right away. Mom's voice drops. "Apologize to Cass this minute, Paul! Apologize, or go to your room!"

"Oh no, it's okay!" Cass says, but I'm up and out of there like a rocket.

I lie on my bed, staring at the spot on the ceiling, hands under my head. I hear their voices in the other room, James's deep one, Mom's high-pitched one, Cassie's. They're talking, laughing. They don't even know I'm gone! She's here just a few hours and already she's moved in on *my* family—my mom, my stepdad, even my baby sister!

"Paul?" It's Cassie at the door, knocking. I'd have thought James might come or Mom—not her.

"Go away!" I tell her.

"Please, can I talk to you a second?" she says.

"Go away!"

"Not till you let me apologize."

Apologize? Her? What's this about? Curious, I go to the door and open it.

"What do you want?" I ask. I block the door so she can't come by.

"I just want to say I'm sorry," she says. "I always seem to be saying that. I didn't mean to cause trouble between you and your mom and my dad."

"Yeah, well . . ." I'm thrown off balance. "I shouldn't have said what I did. It's not easy for you either."

"No." She looks beyond me. I can see she'd like to come in, but I stand my ground.

"Janet's nice; I didn't want to like her but I do. You're really lucky. I really miss Dad. I guess I've got to get along with all of you if I want any time with him." She turns away. "That's all I wanted to say."

I get a knot in my stomach, like the way I feel when I've got to spend a day with my father. It's hard to reconnect. Usually, I haven't seen him in a while. Usually, I have to share him with some lady friend and *her* kids. That's how it must be for Cass. Poor kid. She's smarter and more grown-up than I thought.

"Hey, Cassie, wait!" I grab her arm and pull her back. Maybe we *can* be friends.

"What?" She resists me, not quite sure what I'm up to.

"Come in my room a minute. I bought a new CD yesterday." I lead the way into my room and right away go to my player. As if it doesn't really matter I ask, "You know much about Lincoln High?"

"A little." She sits on the floor, with her back against my bed.

"What's it like? How did you make new friends?"

"Well . . ." she says . . . and suddenly, she's talking like we've known each other all our lives.

And I'm listening.

CALLING JACK KETTLE

NORMA FOX MAZER

Meadow wanted to call Jack Kettle. That is, she wanted Jessie to call, but not say who she was or who she was calling for. Meadow had seen him behind the counter one day at the Clubhouse. She hadn't stopped talking about him since. How good-looking he was. What a sweet smile. What a great build.

"Etcetera, etcetera," Jessie broke in. They were upstairs in Meadow's room. "I'm past the stage of making anonymous calls to boys. You should be past it too, Med."

"Jessie!" Meadow's little pale face flamed. "You know how I am."

"Shy," Jessie sighed.

"Massively shy."

"What if you just talk to him at the Clubhouse?" Jessie asked.

"Do what?" Meadow sounded shocked.

"What if I make the call, but you talk to him?"

"Jessie. . . ."

"What if I get things started, then hand you the phone?" She didn't even wait for Meadow's protest.

e just dialed his number. Why not? She'd been speaking for Meadow ever since they became best friends, way back in kindergarten.

"Hello?"

"Jack Kettle, please," Jessie said.

"Speaking."

"Ahh, Jack . . ." Jessie cleared her throat and dropped her voice to what she hoped was a low, fascinating drawl. "How fortunate I found you in. I have a message for you. Someone I know thinks you are very interesting."

"You mean you?" Jack asked.

"If I meant myself, Jack, I would say so."

He laughed. "You sound cute."

Meadow was breathing warmly on Jessie's neck. "Jack," Jessie said. "Believe me, I'm not your type."

"This other girl, is she pretty?"

"Is that all that matters to you guys? However, if you must know, yes, she's pretty. Blonde, with big brown eyes, plus she's smart and athletic. Plus, she has an adorable mole near her mouth."

"Ssss." Meadow dug her chin warningly into Jessie's shoulder.

"She's blonde?" Jack asked.

Jessie sighed. Didn't he hear anything else she'd said? "Tell me something, Jack. Why do you boys always get excited about blonde girls?"

He laughed again. "I don't know. What's this mystery girl's name?"

"Now, now, Jack. That's a secret. I'll give you a hint, her first initial is M."

"Marylee Farber?"

"Don't you wish." Marylee was a senior who had been prom queen last year and who was a shoo-in for valedictorian this year.

"Melody Farmer?"

"No, Jack."

"Misty Alzicia? Margaret—"

"Wrong, wrong, again. Bye, bye. No more guesses."

Jessie put the phone down.

"You told him about my mole." Meadow lightly touched the corner of her mouth. "He's going to know who I am."

"Is that the thanks I get for doing your dog work?" Jessie demanded.

"What do you want me to do?" Meadow asked.

"Grovel at my feet. Say I'm a wonderful friend."

"You're a wonderful friend."

Jessie smiled modestly. "I know."

The next time they called Jack Kettle, they were in Jessie's house. A woman answered the phone. "Could I speak to Jack, please?" Jessie said.

"Who's calling?" his mother asked.

"Aaah, a friend," Jessie said.

"Just a moment . . . Jack!"

"Jessie, was that his mother?" Meadow whispered.

"I think so, Meadow."

"How did she sound?"

"Like a mother, Meadow."

"Hello?" Jack said.

"Jack! This is your mystery friend, speaking on behalf of MBC, or should I say the fabulous MBC," Jessie said.

"Is that for Most Beautiful Creature?"

"Very good, Jack!"

"What school do you go to?" Jack asked.

"That's for me to know, and you to wonder, Jack. You know nothing about me, and that's the way it should be. I, however, sort of know what you look like, where you work, and—"

"You're giving him too many clues," Meadow whispered harshly.

"When am I going to meet you in person?" he said. "You sound so cute. And your voice! Good voice!"

"Did you ever hear a bad voice? Don't bother answering. I am not cute. And now, you're thinking, If she's not cute, why am I talking to her?"

"I'm not thinking that!" Jack said.

"Sure you are," Jessie said. "Goodbye, I'm tired of talking to you."

"Why did you hang up on him, Jessie?"

"Because I felt like it, Meadow. He was boring me. Why are we whispering?"

The third call to Jack Kettle was from a phone booth in front of a gas station on Nottingham Road. "I wouldn't do this for anyone but you," Jessie said.

"I know." Meadow put her guitar case down.

"Prepare for disappointment," Jessie added instructively. "He was home the first two times; he won't be home this time. Law of averages, Meadow."

Jack Kettle answered on the first ring.

Meadow stuck her tongue out at Jessie.

"Hey, it's the girl with the voice," Jack Kettle said.

"Hey, it's the boy with the laugh."

He laughed.

"Did you ever think," Jessie said, "that our planet is like a huge sprawling house, and we humans are like the family that moved in and forgot to pay the rent."

"Hey!"

"When the family moved in, they had more rooms than they would ever need. So they thought, Jack. Which is why they didn't bother cleaning up their messes. If a room got too grotty, they just shut the door and trekked on to a nice fresh room."

"Jessie, what are you doing?" Meadow hissed.

Jessie continued. "A long time passed, Jack, and they started having trouble with the house. The plumbing wasn't the greatest anymore. The roof was leaking, and nearly every room was in use." She paused. "What do you think about all this, Jack?"

"He doesn't think anything," Meadow said. "He's gone." She had her finger pressed down on the switch. "You were boring him, Jessie." She picked up her guitar case and walked away.

"How do you know?" Jessie said, going after her.

"Because you were boring me! Besides, there

46

wasn't anything about *me* in that conversation."

"Meadow, I can't mention your name, I can't say how you look, I can't say that you know him from the Clubhouse. What am I supposed to say?"

"I don't know," Meadow said.

"Besides, he's a muscle-bound jerk. Why don't you get a crush on someone smart?"

"He's not a jerk!"

"All those guys with muscles are jerks."

"You make me so mad when you say stupid things like that!"

"And you make me mad when you say the things I say are stupid!"

They glared at each other. Then Meadow went one way, toward her guitar lesson, and Jessie went the other, toward the diner where her mother worked.

In the morning, Jessie was in a bad mood. She always was when she and Meadow quarreled. The worst part about it was that today was the annual Save the County Walk. This was the third year Jessie had signed up and, grumpy as she felt, she still wasn't going to miss it. Her mother drove her to the park where the walk started.

Her team consisted of an older man with big square teeth, a couple wearing identical denim outfits, and a boy in baggy striped pants, wearing a camouflage hat pulled down over his eyes.

Jessie started filling up her garbage bag, darting

at every glimmer of glass and metal. There was something gratifying about doing this—the same feeling she had when she attacked her room following a long period of grunge.

The older people had drifted to the other side of the road. They were laughing and having a good time, while she and the boy hadn't said a word. After what seemed like about five hundred minutes of silence, she said to him, "I heard there're a couple hundred people on this walk."

"Uh huh," he said.

Just her luck to be stuck with a brilliant conversationalist. She picked up a slimy piece of plastic. "Two hundred out of a quarter of a million. You'd think a few more would want to save it."

He glanced at her and dipped into the flattened grass for some beer cans.

"This is my third year doing this," she said, trying to talk to him again.

"Hey."

"And it always rains," she said.

"Why?"

"It's a law," she said. "I thought everyone knew. Even though the sun is shining when the walk begins, it has to rain before it's over."

He laughed. Well, that was an improvement.

"How about you?" she said. "How many years have you been going on this walk?"

"My first time," he said.

"Congratulations." For saying three words.

She felt his eyes on her as she rolled a tire toward the road and tagged it for the truck.

"Eight ten-thousandths of a percent," he said all of a sudden.

"What?"

"Two hundred people is eight ten-thousandths of one percent of a quarter of a million."

"You did that in your head?" Jessie asked.

He blushed. "I'm going to study sanitary engineering. Math is useful."

She bent down to clean up some broken glass. He knelt down too, putting them nose to nose. Suddenly he said, "Some eyebrows you have!"

"They're mine," Jessie said.

"I didn't say I didn't like them."

They walked again. This time he started the conversation. "I have an idea that the earth is like a house with a lot of rooms. And humans are the family who live in the house."

Jessie stared at him, speechless for once.

"Do you realize we're using up all the clean rooms?" he asked.

"I think I do," she managed. She'd realized something else too. "Great idea, Jack," she said.

He actually jumped with surprise. "Hey, you know my name?"

"I guess I do." Oh, why torture him? "You work at the Clubhouse, don't you?"

"Did you see me working out on the machines?" he asked hopefully.

Jessie raised one of the eyebrows that awed him. "Oh man. Watching guys work out on machines is not one of my preferred pastimes."

"You're so cute. What's your name?" Jack asked.

"Jessie. Quick, what's yours? Never mind. Just testing." She closed the full garbage bag with a twist-tie and left it by the side of the road for the truck. "So Jack, how did you come up with that idea about the earth being a house?"

"Ahhhh . . . it's actually not my idea." He blushed again. "My ahhh girlfriend's. That is, ah, this girl I talk to on the phone . . ."

Jessie snapped open a fresh plastic bag and just then, the truth was revealed to her. Jack Kettle was not just a bonzo bunch of bulging muscles. Well, he was, but he was more than that. He was also sweet, honest when put to the test, and shy. Definitely shy.

Oh, no. Not another shy person in her life.

"Bad," Jessie mumbled. "Bad, very bad!" She had not only fallen for Meadow's crush, but agreed to meet him in the mall on Monday afternoon. When Meadow found out, she was going to die of heartbreak, and then she was going to kill Jessie.

"Two girls, one boy," Jessie wrote in her notebook. "Jessie. Meadow. Jack." She perked up for a moment, noticing that she and Jack shared the same first initials. So what? Meadow had seen him first. Jessie hadn't even liked him. She had been so sure that all his brains had dripped out of his head and down into his puffy, muscular arms.

Two girls, one boy, one big mouth, she thought gloomily. She flung herself down on her bed and considered her options. She could tell Meadow about Jack . . . or she could not tell Meadow about Jack.

Tell her. Bring her to the mall to meet him. Friendship is stronger than crushes.

That was a noble thought.

Jack would see Meadow and blush. She was so pretty. His face would turn that adorable bright pink. Meadow would gasp and disappear behind Jessie.

Then what?

Neither of them would say a word.

Jessie could see Meadow's face doing a dance of indecision. She could see Jack struggling for words.

Two shy people—that would never work. Don't tell. Meet him at the mall. Have Jack to yourself.

A mean, selfish thought.

She held her head in her hands. It was all up to her. Power, power, power. She could make things happen any way she wanted them to.

Two girls, one boy. Two crushes, one friendship.

She staggered to her feet and stared at herself in the mirror for a long time. She saw a girl with a best friend. She saw a girl with a big crush. She saw a girl who didn't want to give up either one.

She took her lip gloss and drew a house with two windows and in each window, a girl. She made their hands touch. Then, with a little more energy, she drew a boy floating in space outside the house. She put in some stars and the sun and the moon, too, while she was at it. She hoped lip gloss wasn't too hard to get off glass. She drew a heart around the boy. The girls were smiling and looking at him. He was smiling, too.

She stood back and studied her work of art. What else did it need? She considered making the boy into a heart balloon and giving each one of the girls a string to it. But, finally, she did nothing. The picture was fine just the way it was. Two girls, one boy.

DID YOU LIKE THIS BOOK?

Here are two other READ 180 Paperbacks that you might like to read.

JANE EYRE
She has finally found a good job with a nice family. But who—or what—is making scary sounds at night and setting fires in the house?!
BY TRINA ROBBINS. BASED ON THE NOVEL BY CHARLOTTE BRONTË

SUMMER ON WHEELS
Hector and his *amigo* Mando are looking for adventure as they set out on a bike trip from their neighborhood in East Los Angeles to Santa Monica.
BY GARY SOTO